Copyright © 2013 by Beau Holwick.
Illustrations copyright © 2013 by Breeze Kruse
Edited by Beau & Eben Holwick
All rights reserved. This book or any portion thereof may not be reproduced or used in any manner whatsoever without the express written permission of the publisher except for the use of brief quotations in a book review.

Library of Congress Control Number: 2013954639
Cataloging in Publication Data available upon request

Second Printing, 2015
Printed in China

ISBN 978-0-9910184-0-6

Beauness Innovations
1748 Lewis River Rd.
Woodland, WA 98674
www.bailybug.com
beaunessinnovations@gmail.com

Baily Bug

(Baily-Roly-Butter-Poly-Fly-Hopper-Bee)

A Story of Self-Acceptance

Written by Kerri Brown Illustrated by Breeze Kruse

We would like to say thank you to all those who have believed in us and helped us to make this book a reality.

A special thanks to Kip, Kenny, Kelly, Kim, Konny, and Kathy.
Also a special thanks to Bruce & Debbie Devine,
Vera Bennett, and Desiree Flake.

To my Baily Bug, Baily Fay - Grandma KB

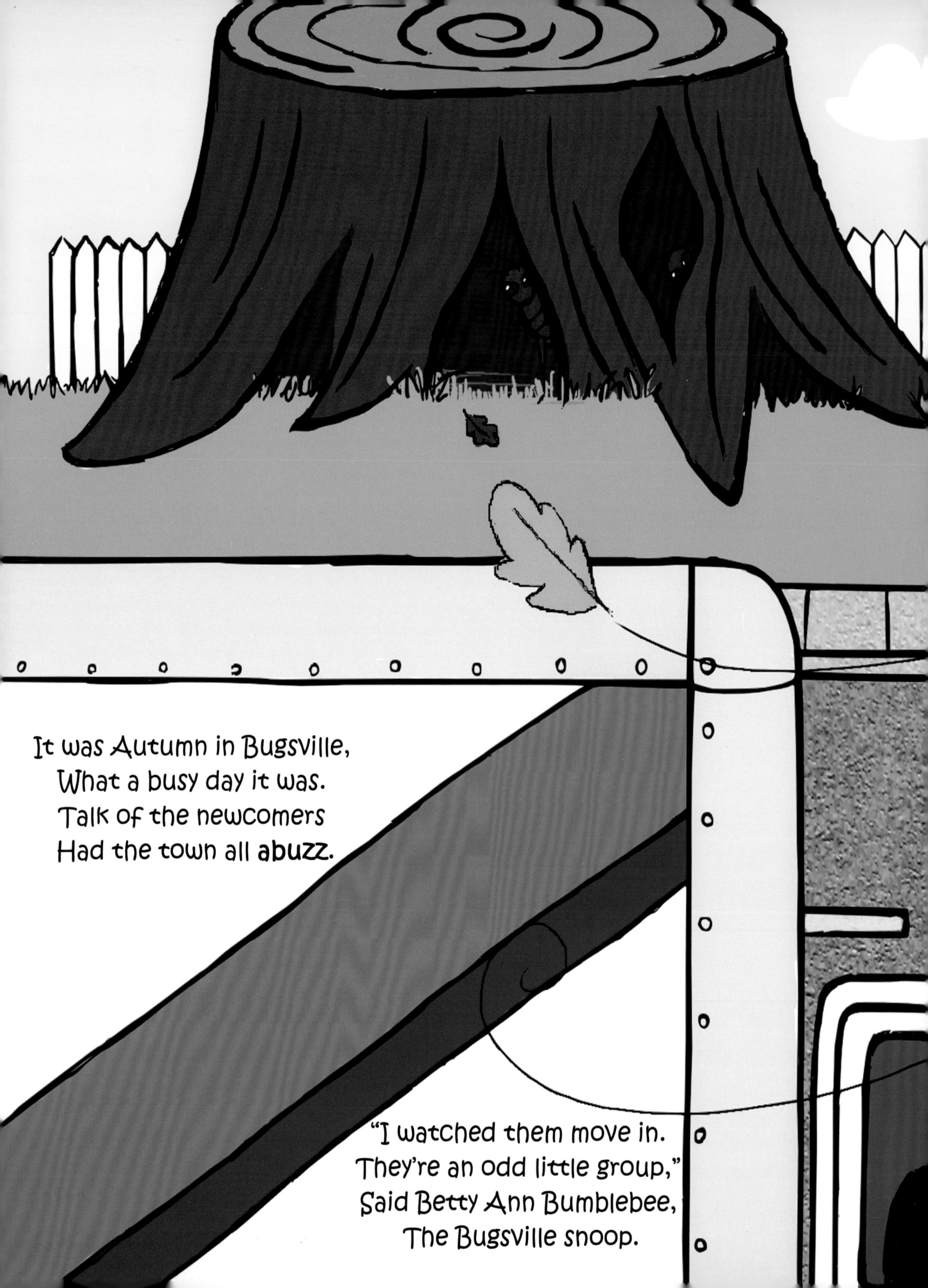

It was Autumn in Bugsville,
What a busy day it was.
Talk of the newcomers
Had the town all **abuzz**.

"I watched them move in.
They're an odd little group,"
Said Betty Ann Bumblebee,
The Bugsville snoop.

"I don't even know what kind they are.
They're the strangest bugs I've seen by far!"
All morning long the town folk **chattered**
Until off to work and school they scattered.

Miss Molly Millipede told
The class, "Settle down!
We have a new student
Who just moved to town.
Let's give a warm welcome,"
Teacher said with a grin,
As the new little bug
Slowly walked in.
Miss. M.
Class Rules

The students started giggling
As she came into view.
Little Lucy Ladybug said,
"Ew! What are you?"
The teacher was friendly,
"Put your lunch on the shelf,
Then please come up front
And introduce yourself."

"I'm Baily Roly-Butter-Poly-Fly-Hopper-Bee,
But just call me Baily Bug, that's fine with me."
Her classmates were laughing and started to poke fun,
When Miss Molly scolded, "That's enough everyone!"
s. M.
Ha Ha
Ha Ha

Baily was sad and as she walked to her desk,
She kept her eyes on the floor and her chin to her chest.
She thought to herself, "Here we go again,
Another new school where I don't fit in."
Ha Ha
Ha Ha

At recess her classmates played all sorts of games,
But not with Baily, they just called her names.
"Baily Whatcha-callit," came from Frankie Firefly.
Kenny Katydid called her, "Baily Who-Am-I."
All through the day she was teased and **taunted**.
Just to have friends was all Baily wanted.

When Baily got home Mommy Bug could tell
That her daughter's day didn't go very well.
Mommy gently wiped Baily's tear-stained cheeks.
The little bug cried out, "They think I'm a freak!"
"Now, now," Mommy soothed as she held Baily's hand,

"Some kids can be mean when they don't understand."
Mom added, "You're special," giving Baily a hug,
"You're not an average-everyday bug."
"I don't want to be special," Baily Bug wailed!
"I'm over the top on the Freak-a-zoid Scale!"

The next day at school Baily sat all alone
While the others had fun in the playground **zone**.
Nobody picked her to be on their team,
And nobody offered to share a swing.
"You look so weird," Adley Ant **declared**,
As the other young bugs whispered and stared.

All through the fall
And into the winter,
Baily couldn't find one
Bug to **befriend** her.

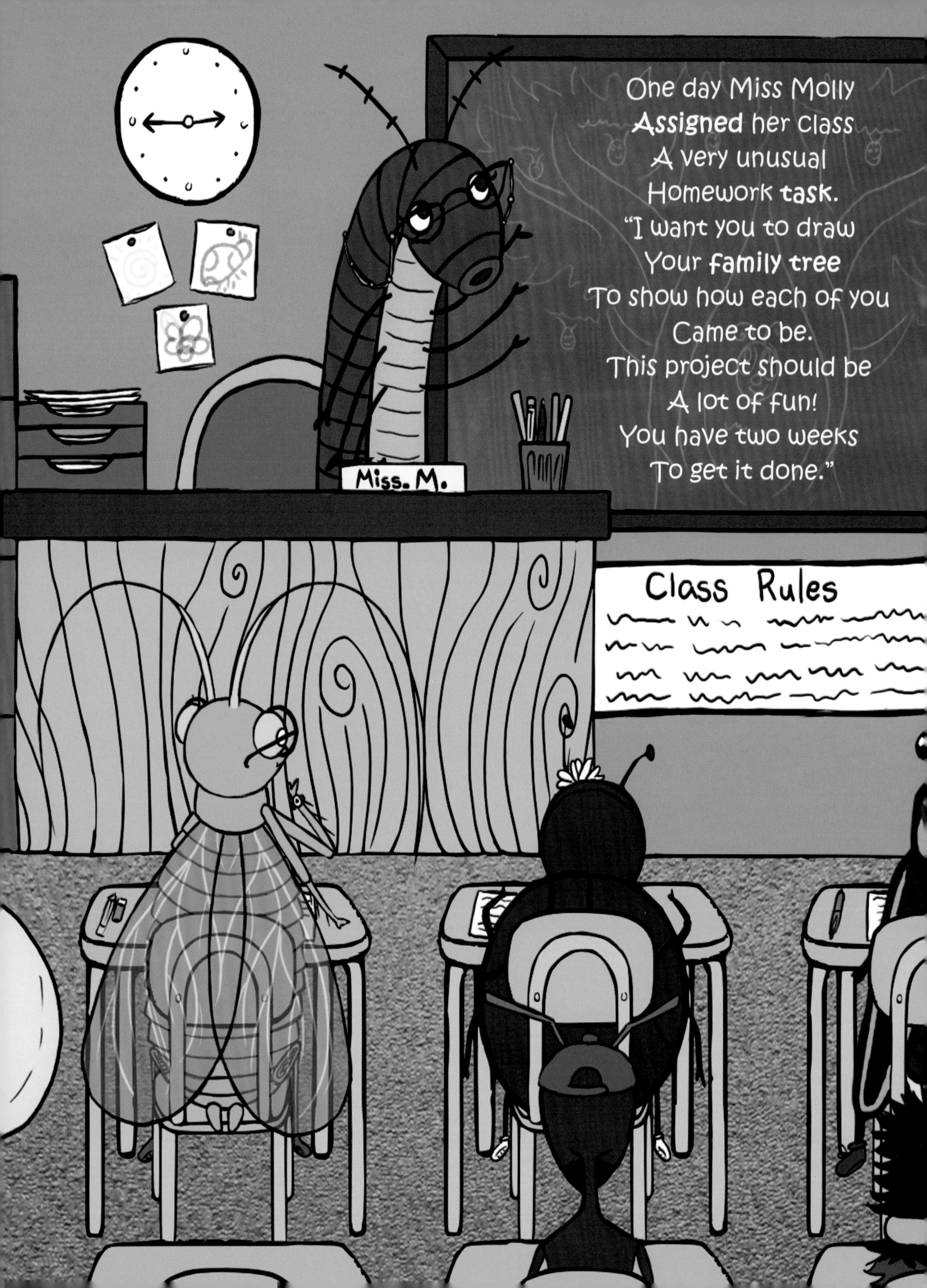
One day Miss Molly
Assigned her class
A very unusual
Homework task.
"I want you to draw
Your family tree
To show how each of you
Came to be.
This project should be
A lot of fun!
You have two weeks
To get it done."
Miss. M.
Class Rules

X 1 2 3 4 5 6 7
1 1 2 3 4 5 6 7
2 2 4 6 8 10 12 14
3 3 6 9 12 15 18 21
4 4 8 12 16 20 24 28
5 5 10 15 20 25 30 35
6 6 12 18 24 30 36 42
7 7 14 21 28 35 42 49
8 8 16 24 32 40 48 56
Baily Bug said to herself, "Oh, no!
That's the last thing
I want anyone to know!
When the kids find out
To whom I'm related
And how on earth I was created,
I'll never make friends!
I'm **doomed** for sure!
How much **humiliation**
Can an insect **endure**?!"

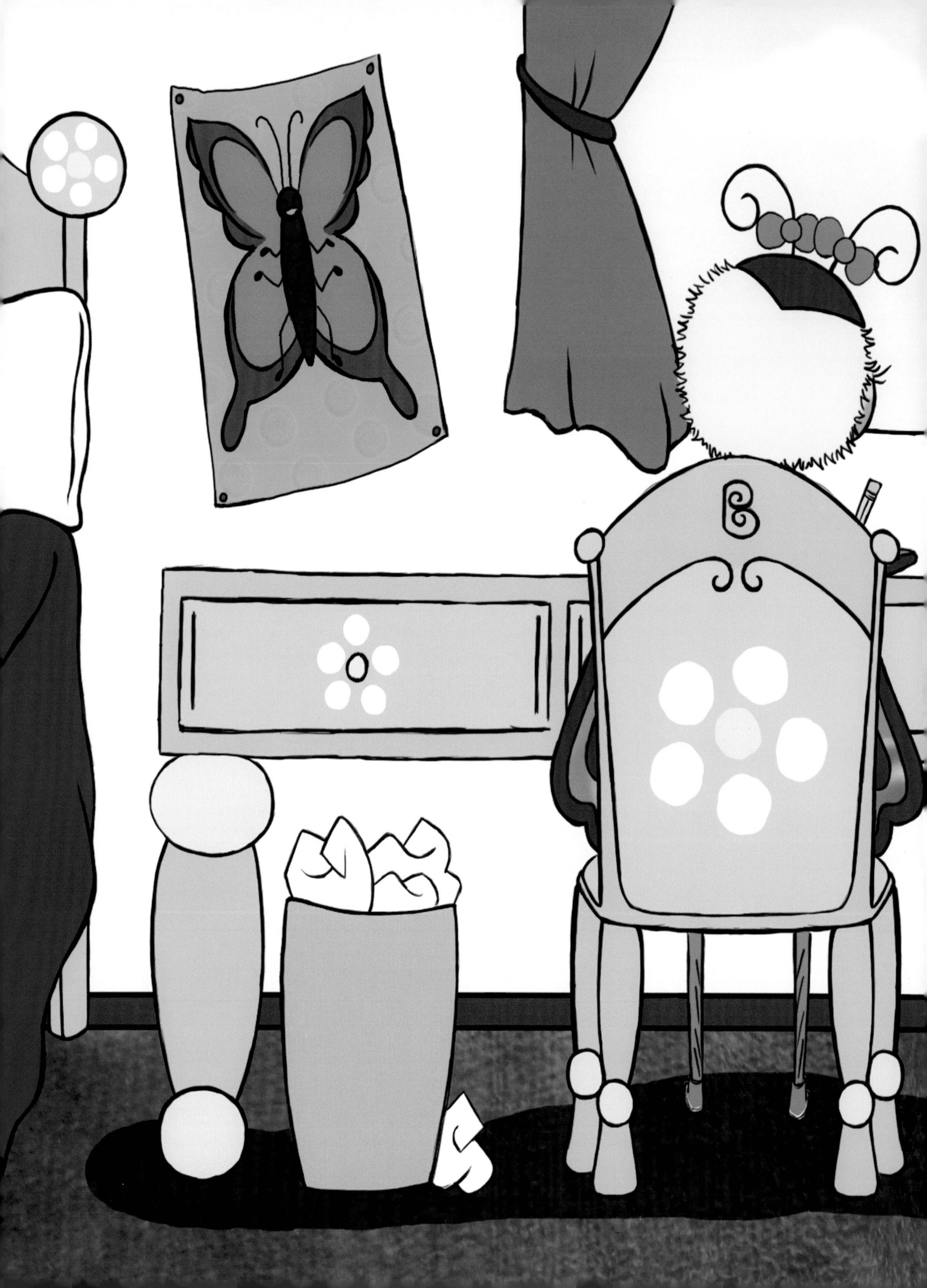

All through the week
And into the next
Baily wrote and re-wrote
Her family tree text.
An exaggeration there, a little lie here,
Would help to make her family appear
Much more normal like all of the others
Who have regular fathers and regular mothers.

Finishing her work,
Baily let out a yawn,
Then decided to go play
In her fort on the lawn.
But before she could leave
She heard Daddy shout,

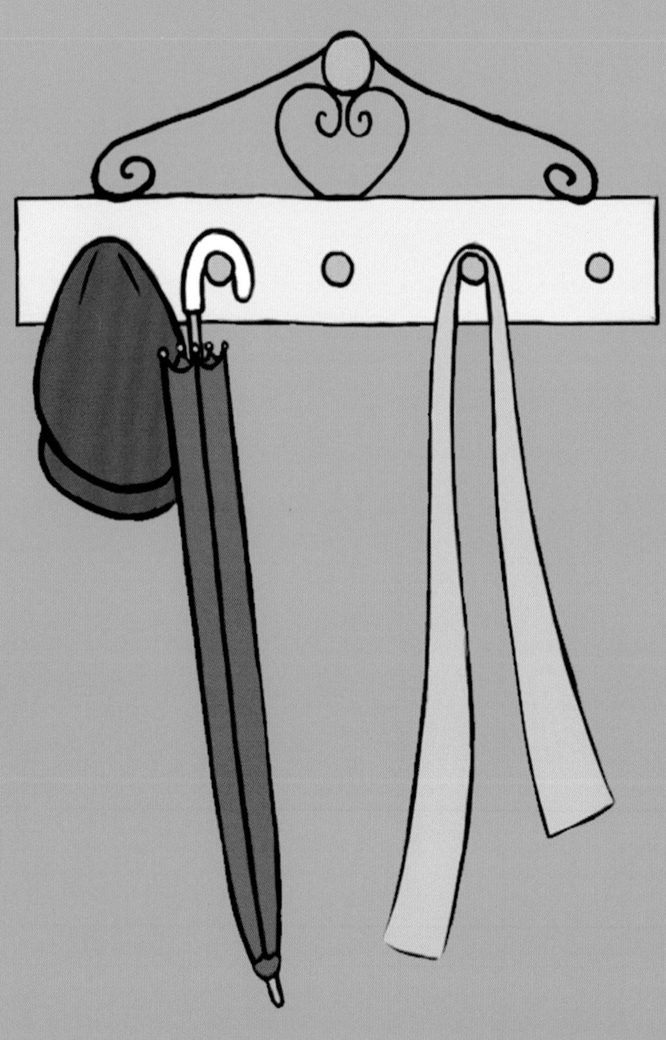

"How did your
Family tree turn out?
We'd like to see it,
If you don't mind."
"Aw, Dad! Do ya hafta?"
Baily Bug whined.

She knew she was in a bad position
As her parents looked over her **composition**.
Mom shook her head and said with a sigh,
"Why did you feel you had to lie?"
Daddy Bug added, "You should be proud
That you are different than most in a crowd."

"To your mom and me
You're a shining star.
You can change how you feel,
But not what you are."

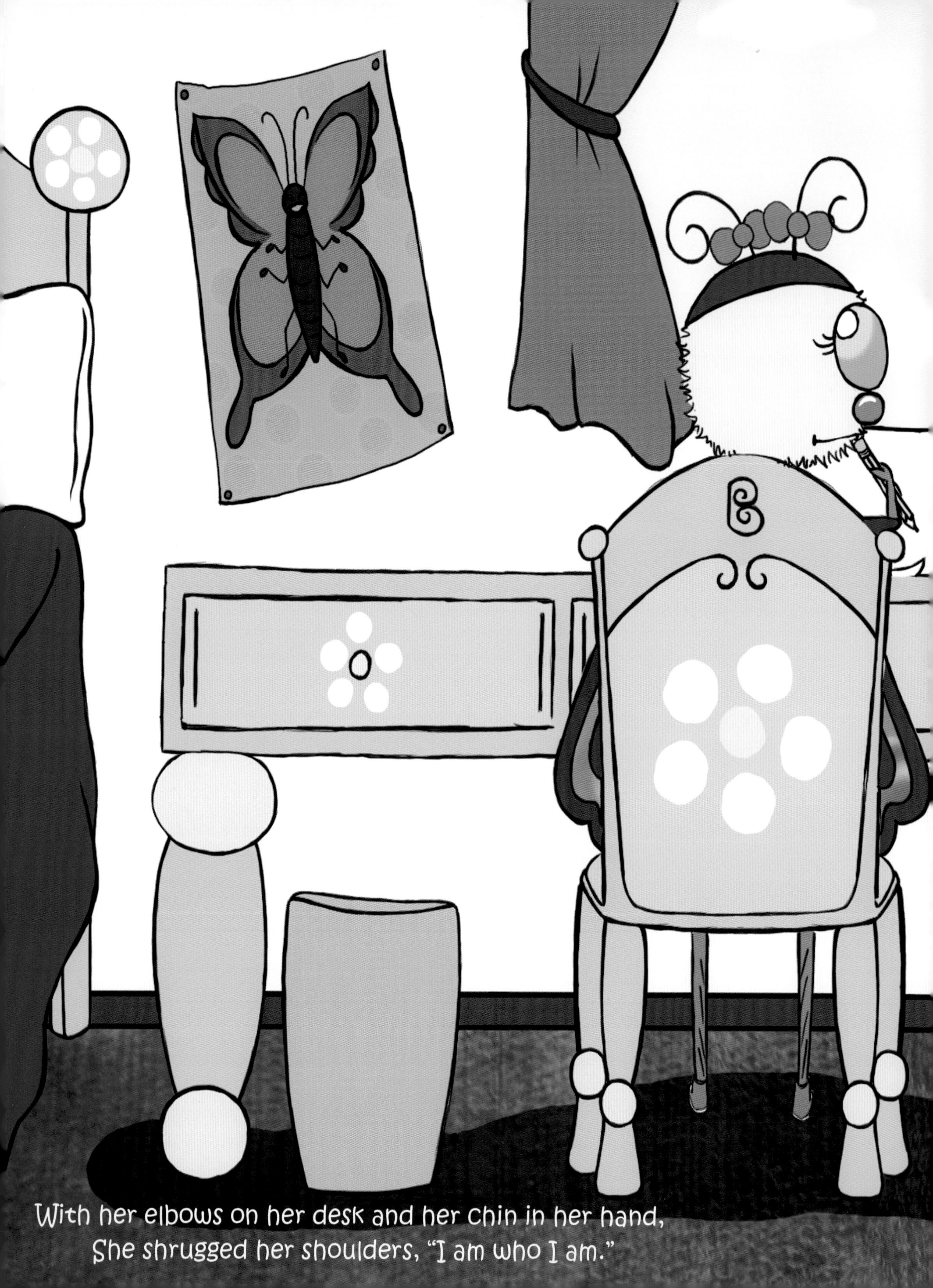
With her elbows on her desk and her chin in her hand,
She shrugged her shoulders, "I am who I am."

So she started all over,
Writing just what was true.
She worked through the
Morning and all afternoon.
When Baily Bug finished
She said with a **smirk**,
"You know, I think
This just might work."

The classroom was filled with sounds of excitement
As the young bugs turned in
Their homework assignments.
Miss Molly explained that she would pick three
To present to the class their **family tree.**
First was Frankie Firefly.
He told how his family could light up the sky.
Miss. M.
Class Rules

Next was Kenny Katydid
Who explained that when he was just a kid
His grandpa, Kyle, taught him to sing
By playing music with his wings.
Miss Molly then chose the last of the three,
"Baily Roly-Butter-Poly-Fly-Hopper-Bee."
Miss. M.
Class

Baily walked slowly
To the front of the room.
Her mind was filled
With thoughts of doom.
"They're going to think
My family is weird.
They'll laugh and be mean,"
The little bug feared.
Miss. M.

Class Rules
X 1 2 3 4 5 6 7
1 1 2 3 4 5 6 7
2 2 4 6 8 10 12 14
3 3 6 9 12 15 18 21
4 4 8 12 16 20 24 28
5 5 10 15 20 25 30 35
6 6 12 18 24 30 36 42
7 7 14 21 28 35 42 49
8 8 16 24 32 40 48 56
She went to the board
And picked up the chalk.
"If it's okay,
I'll draw as I talk."

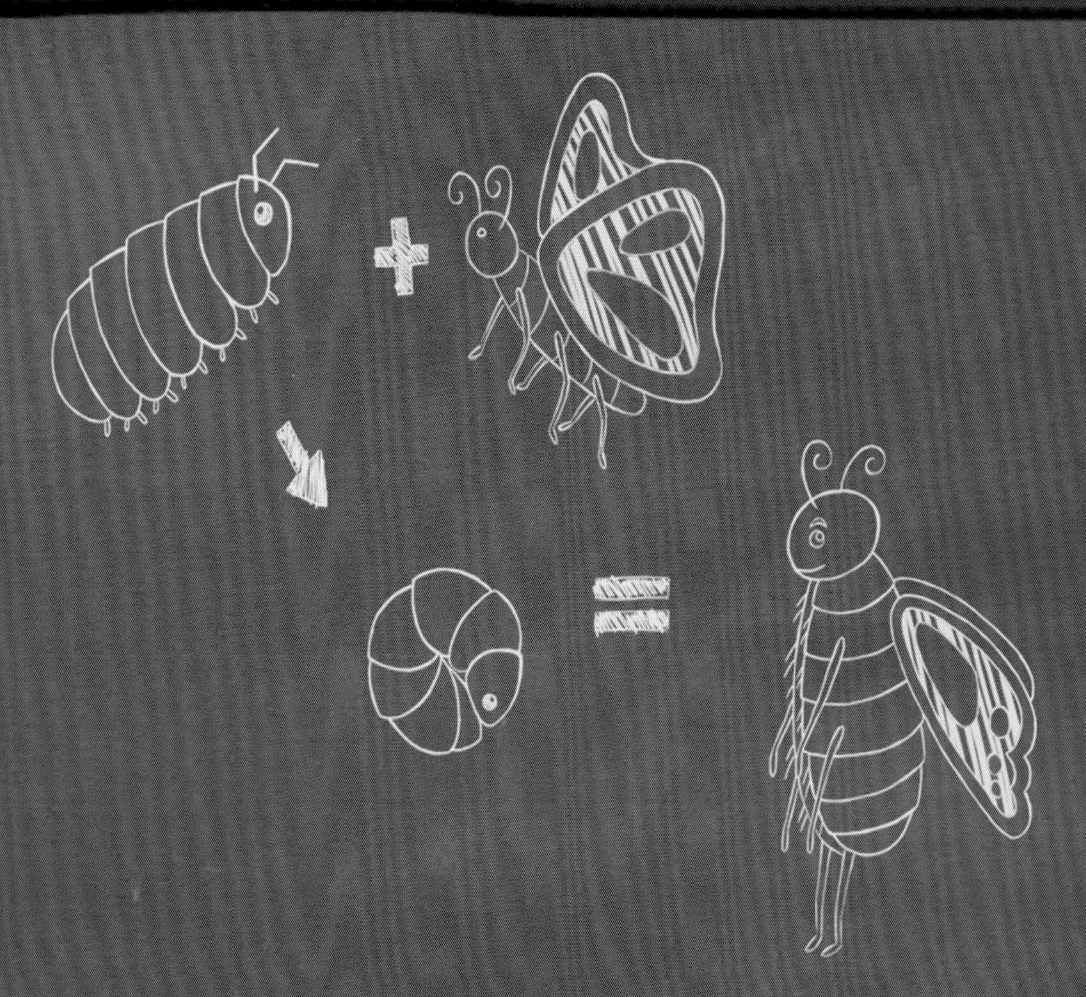

"You'll understand better if my tree's **illustrated**
As I tell you how we're all related.
My daddy's dad can get real small
By curling himself up in a tight little ball.
He's a funny **European** Roly-Poly.
I know what you're thinking – '**Holy Moly!**'"

"When I pull in my wings, my legs and face,
I can roll right through any tight space.
My daddy's mom, I can't deny,
Is a beautiful **Guatemalan** butterfly.
I get my colorful wings from her,
And I can fly high, that's for sure!
That makes my daddy a very rare guy.
He's an interesting Roly-Butter-Poly-Fly."

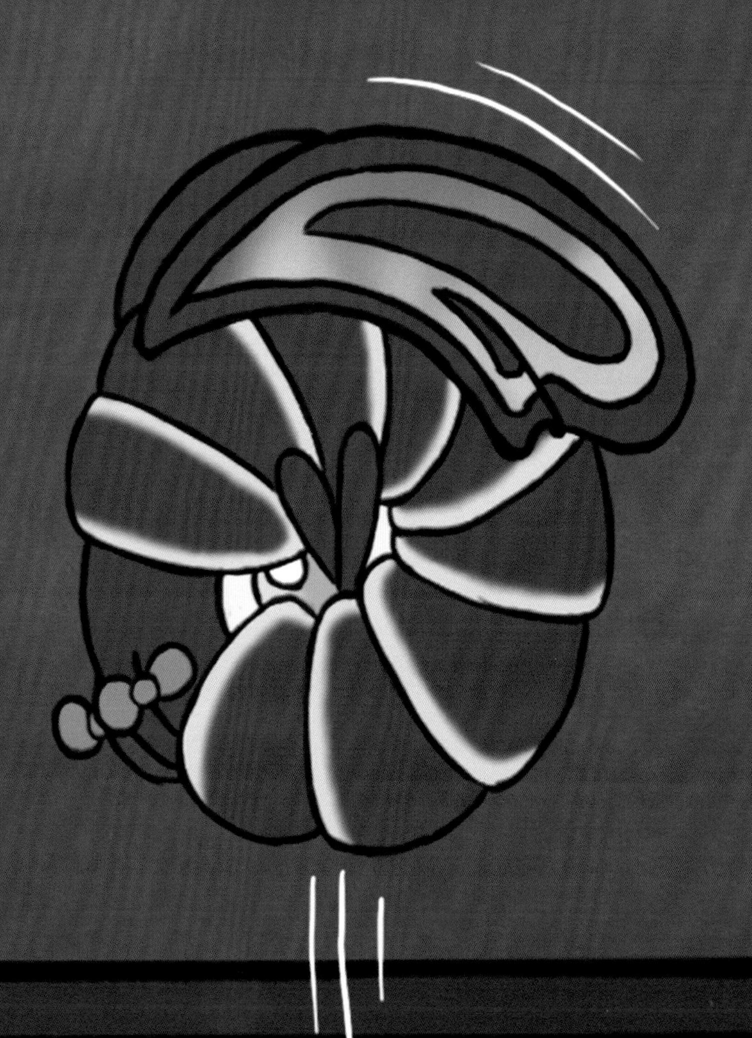

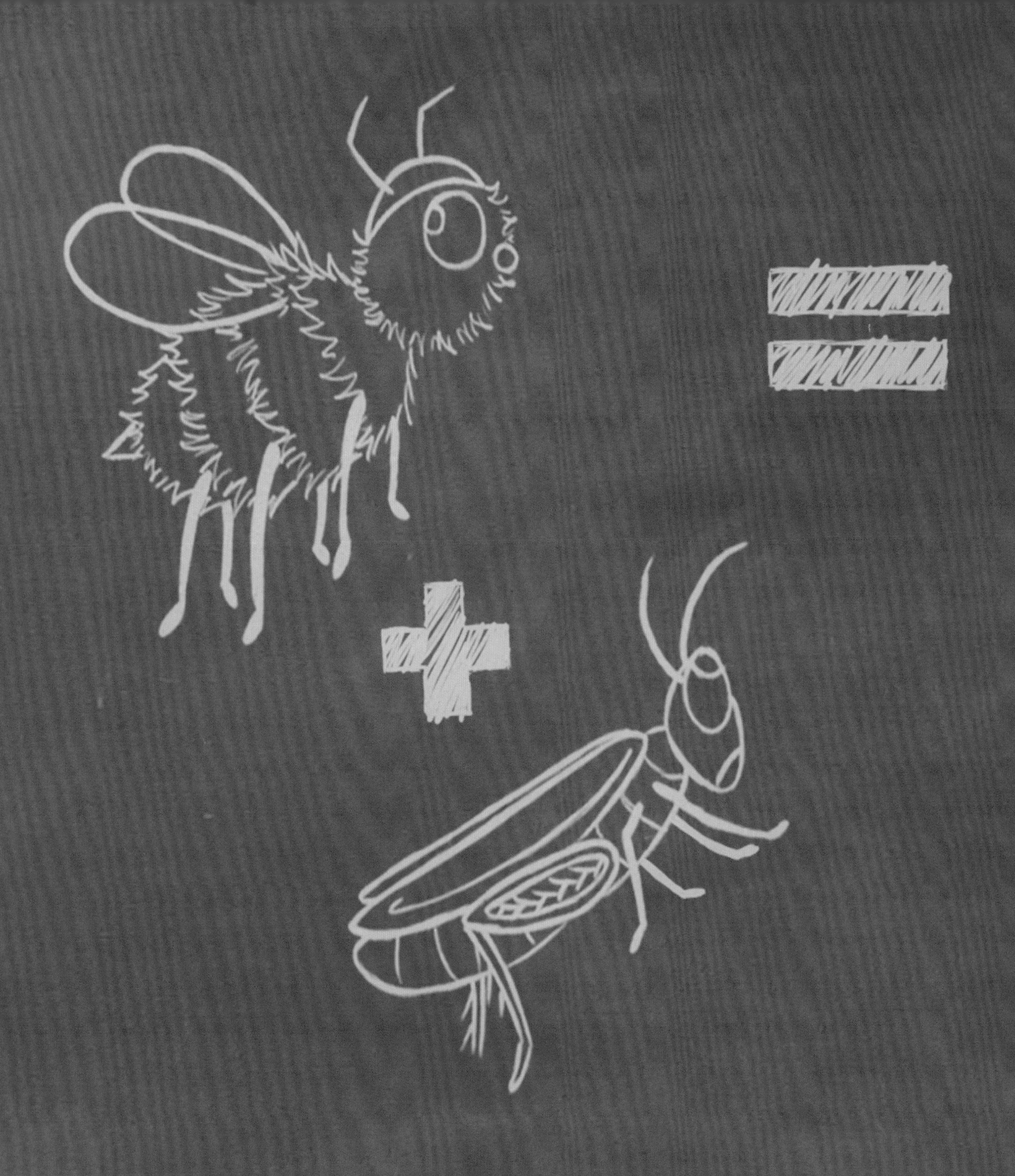

Baily certainly had her classmates' attention,
As they began to see the family **connection**.
She continued on with her family history,
Helping the students **unravel** the mystery.
"The coat I wear, as you can see,
Is like mom's dad, a **Tlingit** Bee."

"My coat keeps me warm when the weather is cold.
He's a very rare type of bee, I'm told.
My mommy's mom is a **German** Hopper.
She can jump so far that no one can top her.
She's who I get my strong legs from.
I can hop, I can skip, I can jump, I can run.
So my mom is called a Hopper-Bee.
No bug is faster or fuzzier than she."

"Now you can see
Why I look like I do.
In so many ways,
I'm just like you.
Greta Grasshopper's
Legs are like mine.
For kicking balls,
They are the best kind."

"Cory Caterpillar
Is soft and furry,
And just like me,
He doesn't worry,
Because we stay warm
While others are freezing,
Wiping their noses,
Coughing and sneezing."

"No bug is better at
Hide-and-seek,"
As she gave Polly Potato Bug
A friendly wink.
"Polly and I are a great design!
We roll up so small
That we're hard to find."

"My wings are a lot
Like Mandy Moth's.
They're colorful and bright
Like **tie-dyed** cloth.
We're great to have
On a baseball field,
Because flying high
Is a useful skill
For catching balls
Being hid by the sun,
That would otherwise be
A scoring home run."

Baily Bug finished and sat back down.
No one was laughing or making a sound.
Wide-eyed and staring, not saying a word,
The students were **processing** what they had just heard.

Then all of a sudden they started clapping!
Baily soon realized what was happening.
They liked her speech! Nothing was wrong!
Adley Ant shouted, "Baily's the Bomb!"

During recess it suddenly seemed
The kids wanted Baily to play on their teams.
As she readied herself to kick the ball,
She **mused**, "Being special is great after all."

Running past first base,
She thought with a grin,
"Although I'm different, I finally fit in!"

*** NOTE TO PARENTS: Although some of these words have more than one meaning, I only used the definition that is relevant to this story. Please discuss the different meanings with your children.***

ABUZZ: Filled with talk or excitement. Example: You are in school when your teacher announces that Baily Bug will be coming to your school today. Before she gets there your classmates are excited and everyone is talking about how much they love Baily Bug. Your class is abuzz with excitement!

ASSIGNED: Gave someone a job or chore to do. Example: Your mom assigned you to take out the garbage.

BEFRIEND: To become someone's friend. Example: If you see a girl sitting all by herself and you go up to talk to her and be nice, you befriended her. You are awesome!

CHATTERED: Meaningless talk. Example: The children chattered on and on about so many silly things that no one could remember what they were talking about.

COMPOSITION: A written assignment. Example: After you finished reading the book, your teacher asked you to write a composition that would explain what you thought about the book.

CONNECTION: How things are related or linked together. Example: I have a connection with my grandpa because he is my mom's dad.

DECLARED: Made a formal announcement. Example: After the football game the announcer declared that the Exterminator's were the winners.

DOOM/DOOMED: Unhappy destiny or outcome. Example: If you don't study for your spelling test, you may have thoughts of failure or doom, or you might say to yourself, "I'm doomed to fail the test!" You should study next time, right?

ENDURE: Suffer through. Example: When you have a new little baby brother and he cries and cries all night, you have to just endure it until he starts sleeping through the nights. Eventually, his cute little face will grow on you and you'll learn to love him!

EUROPEAN: A person or group of people who is native to the continent of Europe. Example: If your next door neighbor moved here from a country called England, he is European. If he lives in America now, he is a Euro-American.

EXAGGERATION: A statement that makes something bigger or better than what it really is. Example: You want your friends to think that you have more books than they do so instead of telling them that you have 15 books, which is the truth, you lie and tell them you have 50 books. That lie is an exaggeration.

FAMILY TREE: An account of a person's family lineage. Ask your parents to help you make your family tree!

GERMAN: A person or group of people who is native to the country of Germany. Example: If your grandmother was born in Germany, she is a German. And if she now lives in America she is a German American. How awesome is that!?

GUATEMALAN: A person or group of people who is native to the country of Guatemala. Example: If your father was born in Guatemala, he is a Guatemalan. If he lives in America he is a Guatemalan American. Cool, right?

HOLY MOLY: An expression that basically means the same thing as "Wow!" or "I can't believe it!" Example: You're playing soccer and you are at midfield. You kick the ball high up in the air and as it comes back to earth, your teammate hits the ball with his head into the goal. The crowd is amazed and someone shouts, "Holy Moly!"

HUMILIATION: Complete embarrassment or shame which makes a person feel lower than everyone else. Example: Everyone in your class but you got question number three on the test right. When your teacher asks you, in front of the whole class, "Why are you the only one who got it wrong?" you might feel humiliation. Hopefully your teacher would never do this but even if she did, no big deal! You may have just incorrectly read the question.

ILLUSTRATED: Drew a picture or chart that helped make something more clear or easier to understand. Example: You are telling your dad about this really cool bike that you want for your birthday. It has all these awesome parts, and you can get it in any colors you want. Your dad doesn't quite understand which bike you are talking about, so you draw him a picture or illustrate the bike so he can make sure and get the right one.

MUSED: Thought deeply about. Example: You and your big sister are fighting over the TV. You said something very mean to her, and your mom overheard you, so she sent you to your room telling you to "Think about what you said to your sister!" While you are in your room, you mused about the things you said to your sister and realized how hurtful your words were.

PROCESSING: Thinking about and coming to understand what someone just said or did. Example: Your dog is whining and standing by the front door. He's looking back and forth at you and then the door. Your brain is processing what your dog is doing so now you understand that he needs to go outside.

SMIRK: To smile in a self-satisfied way. Example: You clean your room without being told. Your mom didn't know you had already done it, so she tells you to go clean your room. You smirk and say, "I already did it." Now if you choose to do this, be ready because your mom will probably get all gushy and squeeze your cheeks and kiss your face because she is so proud of you! Sheesh!

TASK: A job or chore. Example: On the chore chart your task is to feed the cat twice a day.

TAUNTED: Teased and made fun of. Example: One of your neighbors is a girl who is a little chubby. Some of the kids taunt her by calling her names like "Fatty". Thank goodness you're around to tell the mean kids to stop. Then you ask her to come and play with you. You're a kind person.

TIE-DYED: A way of making a pattern on cloth by tying up pieces of the cloth and then soaking the cloth in dye (permanent coloring). When you take out the ties, those pieces are not dyed. Example: I grew up in the 1960's and 1970's and it was very popular to tie-dye our t-shirts. Maybe your grandparents have pictures of themselves wearing tye-dyed clothing. If they show those pictures to you, be sure to say "Far-Out!" and "Groovy!" I promise, they will understand!

TLINGIT (also spelled and pronounced TLINKIT): A member of a group of American Indians who are from the islands and coast of southern Alaska. My son's and daughter's dad is Tlingit Indian. He used to live in Sitka, Alaska. My kids' great-grandfather carved totem poles. Pretty neat, right?

UNRAVEL: To clear up something that was not understood. Example: Your grandmother was born in Germany and your Grandpa was born in Spain, but they both live in the United States. You don't understand how they got to this country. If you ask your grandparents, they can help you unravel that mystery by telling you how they came to the Unites States.

ZONE: An area used for a specific purpose. Example: A town or city has many different zones such as a parking zone, where cars park and a business zone, where there are stores and offices.